JUST
A KID
WITH
A
DREAM

JUST A KID WITH A DREAM

Written by Cindy Similien
Illustrated by Jeric Tan

ISBN: 9798651225262

To contact the author, please email:
CSJ Media Publishing
csjmediapublishing@gmail.com

This book is dedicated to Kaliyan Philo Similien,
you are our legacy –
the link between the past and the future.
Auntie Cindy loves you very much!

–

This book is also dedicated to every child
in every corner of the world.
Dream big!

I am just a kid with a dream.
I can be anything I choose to be.
With patience and hard work,
dedication and perseverance,
I can achieve all of my goals and dreams!

I can be a pilot,
and travel all over the world,
from Haiti to Honduras,
from China to Cambodia,
from Italy to India,
from New York to Nigeria.

I can be a botanist,
and learn more about plants.
Or a zoologist,
and study animals and their behaviors.
Or a photographer,
and capture the beauty
that I see all around me.

I can be an architect,
and design places and spaces,
schools and stadiums,
or homes and office buildings
that reach high up in the sky.

I can be a chef,
and prepare tasty gourmet meals.

I can be a police officer,
and protect my community.

I can be a teacher,
and teach students
how to think for themselves,
and help them see the world
in a different way.

I can be a ballerina and dance with grace
across the world's stage.
Or an actor and dazzle the audience with
my shine and imagination.

Or a musician and play any instrument.
Or a singer and belt any tune,
from Opera to Blues,
from Pop to R&B,
from Classical to Country,
and from Rock to Reggae.

I can be a doctor or a nurse.
A lab technician or a scientist,
and discover the cures for diseases.

I can be a writer or a poet,
and transform the world
with the power of my words.

I am just a kid with a dream.
I can be anything I choose to be.
With patience and hard work,
dedication and perseverance,
I can achieve all of my goals and dreams!

About the Author

Cindy Similien is an award-winning Haitian-American author, cultural ambassador, and women & girls empowerment advocate. Her life's motto is: "Live to love; work to improve the lives of others; and create a legacy." She studied English Literature and Creative Writing at Barnard College-Columbia University.